I Wish I Was Sick, Too!

BY FRANZ BRANDENBERG

ILLUSTRATED BY ALIKI

MULBERRY BOOKS • New York

First Mulberry Edition, 1990   1 2 3 4 5 6 7 8 9 10

Library of Congress Cataloging in Publication Data
Brandenberg, Franz. I wish I was sick, too!
Summary: Elizabeth envies her brother the pampered treatment he gets when he is sick in bed. Then she gets sick too.
[1. Envy—Fiction. 2. Sick—Fiction.] I. Aliki. II. Title.   PZ7.B7364Iag [E] 75-46610   ISBN 0-688-09354-X

For Athena, the great wisher,

and Engelbert, the great patient

Edward was sick.

Mother served his meals in bed.

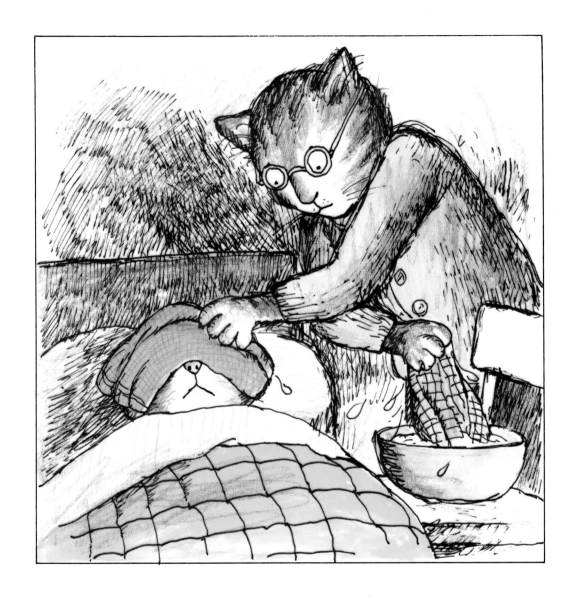

Father made him cold compresses
to bring the fever down.

Grandmother read him stories
to pass the time.

Aunt Ann and Uncle Peter telephoned
to wish him well.

"It isn't fair!" said Elizabeth.
"I have to get up and dress while Mother
serves Edward his meals in bed.

"I have to make my bed and go
to school while Father makes
Edward cold compresses.

"I have to do my homework and practice the piano while Grandmother reads stories to Edward.

"I have to wash the dishes and feed
the pets while Uncle Peter and Aunt Ann
talk to Edward on the telephone.

"I wish I was sick, too!"

A few days later...

Elizabeth was sick.
Mother served her meals in bed.

Father made her cold compresses
to bring the fever down.

Grandmother read her stories
to pass the time.

Aunt Ann and Uncle Peter
telephoned to wish her well.

In the evening Edward came
to tell her what he had done all day.
He had got up and dressed.
He had made his bed and gone
to school.
He had done his homework and
practiced the piano.
He had washed the dishes and
fed the pets.

"It isn't fair," said Elizabeth.
"You are so lucky to do
 all those things."
"I hope you'll be well soon!"
 replied Edward.

A few days later
Elizabeth was well.

She got up and dressed.
She made her bed and went
to school.
She did her homework and
practiced the piano.
She washed the dishes and
fed the pets.

That night Edward and Elizabeth
telephoned Aunt Ann and Uncle Peter
to tell them they were well.

Then they each read a story to
Grandmother to pass the time.

And, as a surprise,
they served their parents
their after-dinner snack in bed.

"The best part of being sick
is getting well," said Edward.
And Elizabeth agreed.